Also by Hillary Duncombe

Differently Different as Different Can Be

All rights reserved. No part of this publication may be reproduced, distributed, or transmitted in any form or by any means, including photocopying, recording, or other electronic or mechanical methods, without the prior written permission of the publisher, except in the case of brief quotations embodied in critical reviews and certain other noncommercial uses permitted by copyright law.

ISBN 979-8-98694-690-0

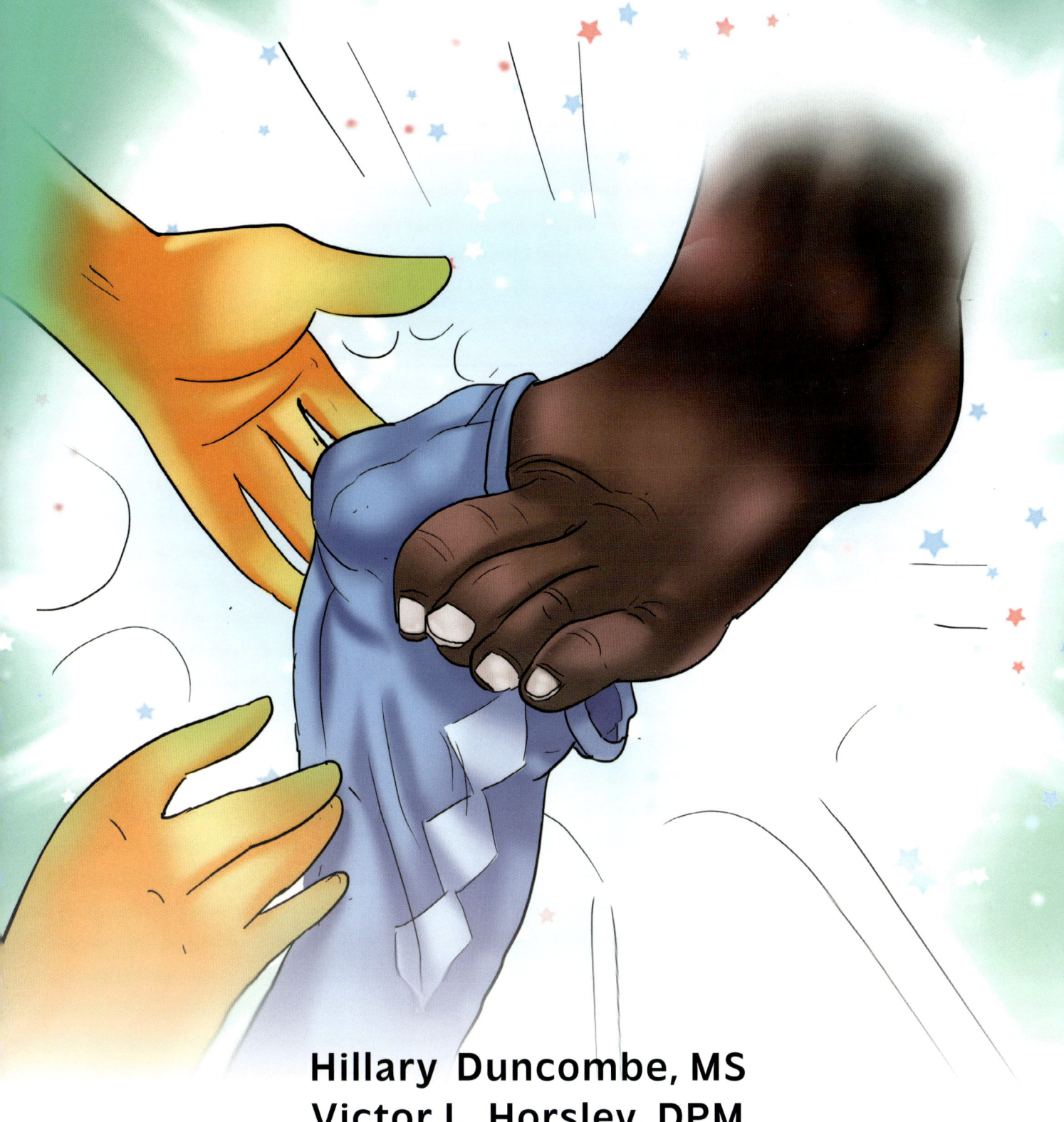

My Toe Can't Go

Hillary Duncombe, MS
Victor L. Horsley, DPM

Acknowledgement

To my dad, daughter, son, and brothers, thank you for your endless love and support. An abundance of gratitude and appreciation to Victor L. Horsley, DPM. When I introduced you to *My Toe Can't Go*, you saw the vision for change in the diabetic community. Your encouragement and willingness to burn the midnight oil with me while adding to this unique and beneficial medical book means so much. DocVic, the name he sometimes goes by, specializes in minimally invasive surgical techniques for the foot and ankle. He is especially fond of spending quality time with his six grandchildren.

To The Doctors

Barton B. Horsley, DPM has over 35-years of experience in diabetic foot and ankle medicine. **Neil L. Horsley, DPM** has practiced since 1985 and has a special interest in foot care for patients with diabetes. **Kairi L. Horsley, DPM** specializes in educating young doctors in surgical residency programs.
Richard H. Mann, DPM is a recognized leader in the treatment of peripheral neuropathy. You are all pioneers in your field, and you bring quality of life and diabetes awareness to communities. Thank you for being available to offer advice.

Recipe Idea

The pineapple's body is hard. There are prickly long leaves on the top of its head. In the Bahamas, some natives bake scrumptious pineapple tarts. Another way to eat pineapples is by adding them to a sweet potato crust pizza with avocado slices and cashew cheese.

Recipe Idea

Did You Know?

Vegetable burgers can be delicious too. Have you ever tried a plant-based burger? Portobello mushrooms make great burgers. You can grill them during your next BBQ. Sauté them with onions and garlic. Season them with your favorite spices and fry them in coconut oil.

So good, enjoy!

PineappleArielle: We are having a "Bring Your Favorite Person to School Day" and you are my most favorite person in the whole wide world.

Activity

Who is your favorite person in the whole wide world?

What can you say or do to let them know how much you love them?

GrammyBurger: Oh! Thank you, Baby. I would love to be there, but Grammy's toe just can't go.

GrammyBurger: Oh, Child! Please look at my toe and tell me what you see. Grammy's eyes are bad and my vision is blurry. I just don't see things the way I used to anymore.

Activity

See if you can find the multi-colored hibiscus flowers. These plants are more than just beautiful. Have you ever tried a hibiscus avocado crunch salad? Here's how to make it– Saute a few hibiscus flowers in avocado oil. Then, add fresh avocado slices, cassava chips, and a dash of pink Himalayan salt. Mix it all together and enjoy it with a cool and refreshing glass of hibiscus tea.

Recipe Idea

Pumpkin is a circular yellowish-orange fruit. Challenge yourself to create a delicious pot of Androsian Coconut Pumpkin Soup. Ingredients–Pumpkin, fresh coconut milk, onions, garlic, carrots, cassava, celery, thyme, rosemary, goat pepper, and Himalayan salt. You are going to love it!

PineappleArielle: What, how can that be? It really looks like it hurts a lot. I think you need to see a doctor right away and find out what's going on with that painful–looking big toe.

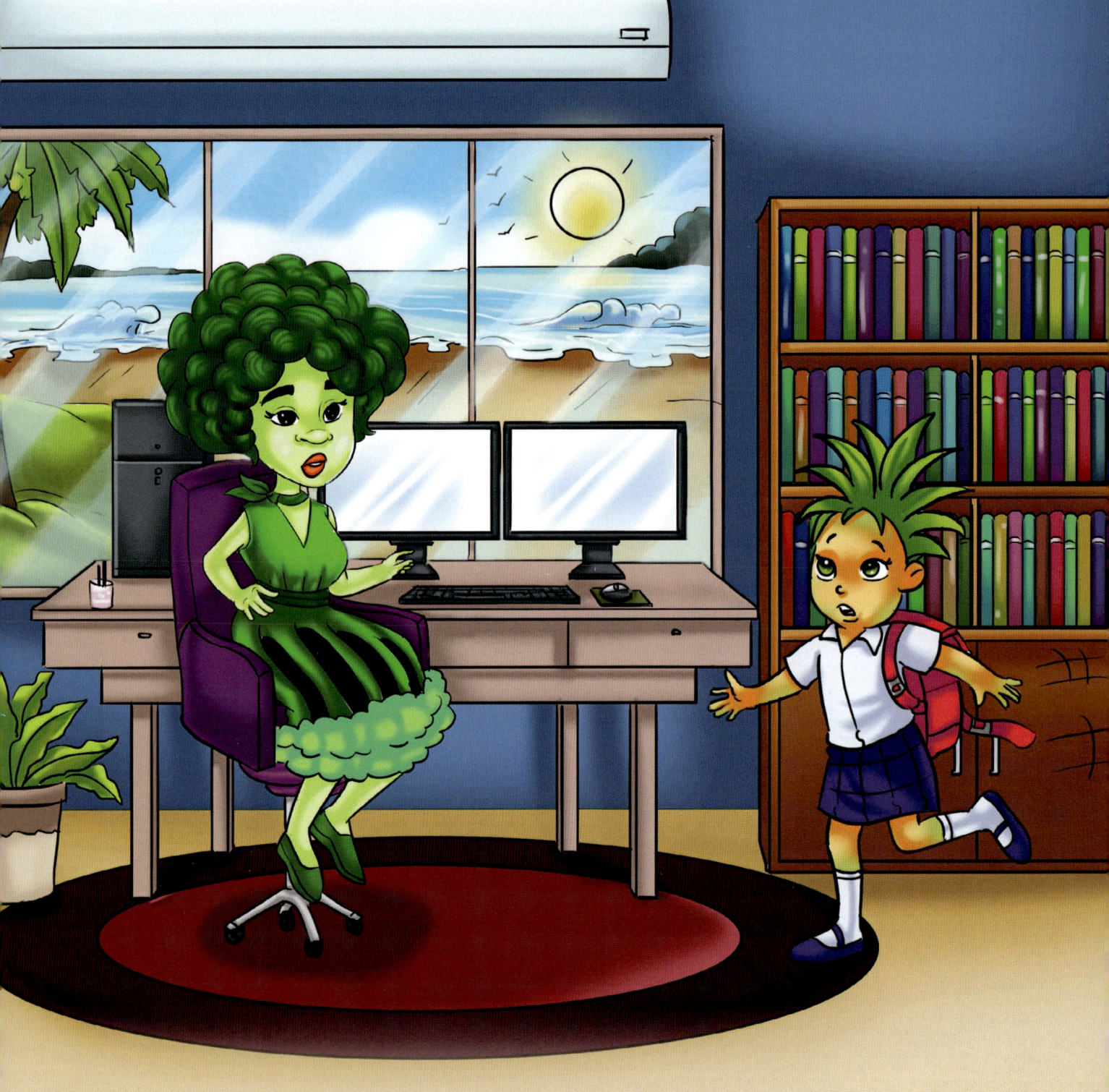

MummyBroccoli: What are you talking about, Baby–girl? Grammy's toe can't go, show me?

MummyBroccoli: Does it hurt?

GrammyBurger: Nope! I don't feel no pain. No pain at all.

Later that day at the hospital...

MummyBroccoli: It's a good thing the podiatrist is able to see your Grammy right away.

PineappleArielle: Podiatrist, I thought you said Grammy was going to a foot doctor.

Vocabulary

Podiatrist: A doctor who takes care of all the foot and ankle problems in the world.

Dr. SugarApple: My name is Dr. SugarApple and I'm your podiatrist. Now let's take a look at this left foot and see what the problem is.

PineappleArielle: Oh! A podiatrist is a foot doctor.

MummyBroccoli: Yes, Baby-girl you're right. Let's see what the doctor has to say about your grammy's toe.

Dr. SugarApple: Okay, I examined GrammyBurger and she has an infected ingrown nail. She has no pain because of a nerve sensory disorder called polyneuropathy.

PineappleArielle: Poly-knew-what?

Dr. SugarApple: Say it like this, "Poly-Knew-Ropathy".

PineappleArielle: Oh, now I get it! Poly-Neu-Ropathy.

Vocabulary

Polyneuropathy (Poly + Neuro + Pathy)
Polyneuropathy means that some of the nerves go bad and can no longer feel pain. This can happen in the feet and sometimes this happens in the hands too.

Sensory Disorders
Sensory disorders happen when you have polyneuropathy. Also, when there are not enough vitamins B1 and B12 in the body sensory disorders can happen.

Nerves
Nerves are the electrical connection from the brain to the tips of your fingers and toes.

Infected
Infected or infection is when a part of the body shows redness, swelling, and sometimes has a stinky smell.

Ingrown Nail
An ingrown nail is a toenail that grows into the skinfolds in a bad way causing pain and possible infection.

Diabetes
A person with diabetes has too much sugar circulating in the blood.

Circulating
Movement of blood within the body.

Amputation
When a doctor cuts off a part of the body, it is called amputation. One body part that is mostly amputated is the big toe.

Dr. SugarApple: Yes, Polyneuropathy is a sickness in the body that happens when a lot of sugar is circulating in the blood. When too much sugar mixes with the blood, it makes the nerves in the body go bad. Bad nerves can cause no feeling in the fingers and toes. No feeling in the fingers and toes is something that happens to most people who have diabetes. This helps to explain why your grammy's toe is not hurting. Polyneuropathy is a serious problem that leads to serious amputations. In other words, sometimes a podiatrist must cut off a toe that goes bad.

PineappleArielle: Noooo! Doctor, please don't cut off GrammyBurger's toe.

One hour later...

Dr. SugarApple: Great news! We saved GrammyBurger's toe. We removed the ingrown toenail and she's good to go.

MummyBroccoli: Thank you, Dr. SugarApple. I was so worried that my mummy's toe would have to go. I read that there is a diabetic amputation crisis in the Caribbean. I also read that amputation in the Caribbean is the highest in the world. They even talked about how the big toe is the first to go.

Vocabulary

Crisis

A crisis is an emergency.

PineappleArielle: You removed her ingrown toenail just like that, is she okay?

Dr. SugarApple: Yup, just like that. It didn't take too long. First, we put the toe to sleep with a local anesthetic. The anesthetic is a medication that makes your grammy's toe surgery pain-free. After that, both borders of the nail were clipped. Then, the clipped toenails were removed permanently, so they don't hurt GrammyBurger's toe anymore. Finally, I applied antibiotic ointment, elastic tape, and gauze to her toe. Oh! I almost forgot to tell you the most important thing. Before every surgery, we check our patient's vital signs and lab work. Lab work tells the doctor about so many important numbers in the body. Numbers like the glucose level, hemoglobin A1c, and uric acid. That's how I knew that GrammyBurger's ingrown toenail could be fixed.

Vocabulary

Anesthetic

Anesthetic is used to block or stop pain signals in the nerves.

Antibiotic ointment

Antibiotic ointment is used to kill germs on infections.

Hemoglobin A1c

Hemoglobin is a protein that helps the red blood cells to carry oxygen to the muscles and other parts of the body. A1c is a test that tells the doctor how good or bad your blood sugar is doing.

Glucose

Glucose comes from the food we eat. It is the main sugar found in the blood.

Gauze

Gauze is a clean bandage or wrap used to protect an area while keeping infection out of a wound or cut.

Uric acid

Uric acid is a normal part of the urine or pee. When your urine is a darker yellow there is a buildup of uric acid.

Oxygen

Oxygen is the air you breathe to stay alive. It has no color and no smell.

Dr. SugarApple: PineappleArielle, would you like to learn more about these numbers so you can help your grammy at home?

PineappleArielle: You mean I can help GrammyBurger get better so she can attend the "Bring Your Favorite Person to School Day"?

Dr. SugarApple: Yes, you sure can. Look at the Monthly Patient Log Sheet. You and your grammy can study it and fill in the blanks together.

Remember

Help yourself or the person you love to write down their numbers.

PineappleArielle: Dr. SugarApple! Thank you for saving GrammyBurger's toe.

Dr. SugarApple: You are very welcome. Remind your grammy to take the *My Toe Can't Go* book with her to every doctor's visit.

PineappleArielle: MummyBroccoli! MummyBroccoli! Now grammy and I have homework to do every day.

PineappleArielle: GrammyBurger, now your toe can go! I'm so happy you and all of my other favorite people are joining me on this special day.

BrotherBreadfruit: Yay! We're all here together.

BrotherSeagrape: Yay!

Vocabulary

Breadfruit: A circular fruit covered with a thick green bumpy skin. The breadfruit's texture is soft with a nutty, creamy, buttery taste. The taste can be changed based on the seasonings added. This unbelievably delicious fruit can be fried in coconut oil, roasted in the oven or over a bonfire, and even boiled.

Sea grape: Found at the seaside in The Bahamas, much like regular grapes, the sea grape is plump, juicy, and delicious.

MummyBroccoli: Let's all take a photo together.

GrammyBurger: Be careful now. Watch out for my toe. I don't want it to can't go again.

DaddyBigdog: Real talk GrammyBurger, you ain't jokin'.

Dr. SugarApple: Thank you for including me in your family photo.

Everyone! Say, "diabetes and polyneuropathy awareness on three, 1, 2, 3, …"

Activity

IMPORTANT

Remember to write down all of your daily findings in the blank spaces on your patient log sheet.

Take your copy of *My Toe Can't Go* with you to ALL your doctor's appointments.

Look at GrammyBurger's results below. Compare her results with the normal vitals chart. Do you think GrammyBurger's numbers are good or bad?

GrammyBurger's Vitals Chart

- Blood Pressure 180/96 mm/Hg
- Pulse or heart rate 62 beats per minute
- Respiration 16 breaths per minute
- Temperature 98.6°F (Fahrenheit)
- HgA1c 7.5% and fasting (did not eat) Blood Glucose 180 mg/dL

Normal Adult Vitals Chart

- Blood Pressure normal 120/80 mmHg over 50-years-old 150/90 mmHg
- Respiration normal (rate of breathing) 12–16 breaths per minute
- Pulse normal 60–100 beats per minute
- Temperature 97.8°F to 99°F (Fahrenheit)
- Random Blood Glucose (RBG) fasting/did not eat less than 100 mg/dL
- RBG before meals 70–100 mg/dL 1–2 hours after eating less than 200mg/dL

Hemoglobin (HgA1c) or a 3-month blood sugar value

- Around or below 6% (115 mg/dL) 6.3 mmol/L (ideal)
- Up to 8% (180 mg/L) 10 mmol/L (not so good)
- 9%–14% (215–380 mg/L) 11.9–21.1 mmol/L (bad)

Practice Writing a Normal Vitals Chart

- Blood Pressure _____/_____
- Pulse _____
- Respiration _____
- Temperature _____
- HgA1c–Hemoglobin _____ % and fasting/did not eat
- Blood Glucose _____ mg/dL

Name: _____

Month: _____

Year: _____

Weight: _____

This Month's Goals...

_____

_____

_____

Are You Drinking Enough Water?

Challenge yourself! Mark a raindrop each time you drink more water.

Great job

Keep going

You did good

Drink more next month.
Exercise and stretch daily.
Limit the suger you eat and drink.

MONTHLY PATIENT LOG SHEET

Day	✓	Pulse	Blood/Pressure	Temperature	Blood sugar 1	Blood sugar 2
1			/			
2			/			
3			/			
4			/			
5			/			
6			/			
7			/			
8			/			
9			/			
10			/			
11			/			
12			/			
13			/			
14			/			
15			/			
16			/			
17			/			
18			/			
19			/			
20			/			
21			/			
22			/			
23			/			
24			/			
25			/			
26			/			
27			/			
28			/			
29			/			
30			/			
31			/			

Name: _____

Month: _____

Year: _____

Weight: _____

This Month's Goals…

_____

_____

_____

Are You Drinking Enough Water?

Challenge yourself! Mark a raindrop each time you drink more water.

Great job

Keep going

You did good

Drink more next month.
Exercise and stretch daily.
Limit the suger you eat and drink.

MONTHLY PATIENT LOG SHEET

Day	✓	Pulse	Blood/Pressure	Temperature	Blood sugar 1	Blood sugar 2
1			/			
2			/			
3			/			
4			/			
5			/			
6			/			
7			/			
8			/			
9			/			
10			/			
11			/			
12			/			
13			/			
14			/			
15			/			
16			/			
17			/			
18			/			
19			/			
20			/			
21			/			
22			/			
23			/			
24			/			
25			/			
26			/			
27			/			
28			/			
29			/			
30			/			
31			/			

Name: _____

Month: _____

Year: _____

Weight: _____

This Month's Goals...

_____

_____

_____

Are You Drinking Enough Water?

Challenge yourself! Mark a raindrop each time you drink more water.

Great job

Keep going

You did good

Drink more next month.
Exercise and stretch daily.
Limit the suger you eat and drink.

MONTHLY PATIENT LOG SHEET

Day	✓	Pulse	Blood/Pressure	Temperature	Blood sugar 1	Blood sugar 2
1			/			
2			/			
3			/			
4			/			
5			/			
6			/			
7			/			
8			/			
9			/			
10			/			
11			/			
12			/			
13			/			
14			/			
15			/			
16			/			
17			/			
18			/			
19			/			
20			/			
21			/			
22			/			
23			/			
24			/			
25			/			
26			/			
27			/			
28			/			
29			/			
30			/			
31			/			

Name: _____

Month: _____

Year: _____

Weight: _____

This Month's Goals...

_____

_____

_____

Are You Drinking Enough Water?

Challenge yourself! Mark a raindrop each time you drink more water.

Great job

Keep going

You did good

Drink more next month.
Exercise and stretch daily.
Limit the suger you eat and drink.

MONTHLY PATIENT LOG SHEET

Day	✓	Pulse	Blood/Pressure	Temperature	Blood sugar 1	Blood sugar 2
1			/			
2			/			
3			/			
4			/			
5			/			
6			/			
7			/			
8			/			
9			/			
10			/			
11			/			
12			/			
13			/			
14			/			
15			/			
16			/			
17			/			
18			/			
19			/			
20			/			
21			/			
22			/			
23			/			
24			/			
25			/			
26			/			
27			/			
28			/			
29			/			
30			/			
31			/			

Name: _____

Month: _____

Year: _____

Weight: _____

This Month's Goals...

_____

_____

_____

Are You Drinking Enough Water?

Challenge yourself! Mark a raindrop each time you drink more water.

Great job

Keep going

You did good

Drink more next month.
Exercise and stretch daily.
Limit the suger you eat and drink.

MONTHLY PATIENT LOG SHEET

Day	✓	Pulse	Blood/Pressure	Temperature	Blood sugar 1	Blood sugar 2
1			/			
2			/			
3			/			
4			/			
5			/			
6			/			
7			/			
8			/			
9			/			
10			/			
11			/			
12			/			
13			/			
14			/			
15			/			
16			/			
17			/			
18			/			
19			/			
20			/			
21			/			
22			/			
23			/			
24			/			
25			/			
26			/			
27			/			
28			/			
29			/			
30			/			
31			/			

Name: _____

Month: _____

Year: _____

Weight: _____

This Month's Goals...

_____

_____

_____

Are You Drinking Enough Water?

Challenge yourself! Mark a raindrop each time you drink more water.

Great job

Keep going

You did good

Drink more next month.
Exercise and stretch daily.
Limit the suger you eat and drink.

MONTHLY PATIENT LOG SHEET

Day	✓	Pulse	Blood/Pressure	Temperature	Blood sugar 1	Blood sugar 2
1			/			
2			/			
3			/			
4			/			
5			/			
6			/			
7			/			
8			/			
9			/			
10			/			
11			/			
12			/			
13			/			
14			/			
15			/			
16			/			
17			/			
18			/			
19			/			
20			/			
21			/			
22			/			
23			/			
24			/			
25			/			
26			/			
27			/			
28			/			
29			/			
30			/			
31			/			

Name: _____

Month: _____

Year: _____

Weight: _____

This Month's Goals...

_____

_____

_____

Are You Drinking Enough Water?

Challenge yourself! Mark a raindrop each time you drink more water.

Great job

Keep going

You did good

Drink more next month.
Exercise and stretch daily.
Limit the suger you eat and drink.

MONTHLY PATIENT LOG SHEET

Day	✓	Pulse	Blood/Pressure	Temperature	Blood sugar 1	Blood sugar 2
1			/			
2			/			
3			/			
4			/			
5			/			
6			/			
7			/			
8			/			
9			/			
10			/			
11			/			
12			/			
13			/			
14			/			
15			/			
16			/			
17			/			
18			/			
19			/			
20			/			
21			/			
22			/			
23			/			
24			/			
25			/			
26			/			
27			/			
28			/			
29			/			
30			/			
31			/			

Name: _____

Month: _____

Year: _____

Weight: _____

This Month's Goals...

_____

_____

_____

Are You Drinking Enough Water?

Challenge yourself! Mark a raindrop each time you drink more water.

Great job

Keep going

You did good

Drink more next month.
Exercise and stretch daily.
Limit the suger you eat and drink.

MONTHLY PATIENT LOG SHEET

Day	✓	Pulse	Blood/Pressure	Temperature	Blood sugar 1	Blood sugar 2
1			/			
2			/			
3			/			
4			/			
5			/			
6			/			
7			/			
8			/			
9			/			
10			/			
11			/			
12			/			
13			/			
14			/			
15			/			
16			/			
17			/			
18			/			
19			/			
20			/			
21			/			
22			/			
23			/			
24			/			
25			/			
26			/			
27			/			
28			/			
29			/			
30			/			
31			/			

Name: _____

Month: _____

Year: _____

Weight: _____

This Month's Goals…

_____

_____

_____

Are You Drinking Enough Water?

Challenge yourself! Mark a raindrop each time you drink more water.

Great job

Keep going

You did good

Drink more next month.
Exercise and stretch daily.
Limit the suger you eat and drink.

MONTHLY PATIENT LOG SHEET

Day	✓	Pulse	Blood/Pressure	Temperature	Blood sugar 1	Blood sugar 2
1			/			
2			/			
3			/			
4			/			
5			/			
6			/			
7			/			
8			/			
9			/			
10			/			
11			/			
12			/			
13			/			
14			/			
15			/			
16			/			
17			/			
18			/			
19			/			
20			/			
21			/			
22			/			
23			/			
24			/			
25			/			
26			/			
27			/			
28			/			
29			/			
30			/			
31			/			

Name: _____

Month: _____

Year: _____

Weight: _____

This Month's Goals...

_____

_____

_____

Are You Drinking Enough Water?

Challenge yourself! Mark a raindrop each time you drink more water.

Great job

Keep going

You did good

Drink more next month.
Exercise and stretch daily.
Limit the suger you eat and drink.

MONTHLY PATIENT LOG SHEET

Day	✓	Pulse	Blood/Pressure	Temperature	Blood sugar 1	Blood sugar 2
1			/			
2			/			
3			/			
4			/			
5			/			
6			/			
7			/			
8			/			
9			/			
10			/			
11			/			
12			/			
13			/			
14			/			
15			/			
16			/			
17			/			
18			/			
19			/			
20			/			
21			/			
22			/			
23			/			
24			/			
25			/			
26			/			
27			/			
28			/			
29			/			
30			/			
31			/			

Name: _____

Month: _____

Year: _____

Weight: _____

This Month's Goals...

_____

_____

_____

Are You Drinking Enough Water?

Challenge yourself! Mark a raindrop each time you drink more water.

Great job

Keep going

You did good

Drink more next month.
Exercise and stretch daily.
Limit the suger you eat and drink.

MONTHLY PATIENT LOG SHEET

Day	✓	Pulse	Blood/Pressure	Temperature	Blood sugar 1	Blood sugar 2
1			/			
2			/			
3			/			
4			/			
5			/			
6			/			
7			/			
8			/			
9			/			
10			/			
11			/			
12			/			
13			/			
14			/			
15			/			
16			/			
17			/			
18			/			
19			/			
20			/			
21			/			
22			/			
23			/			
24			/			
25			/			
26			/			
27			/			
28			/			
29			/			
30			/			
31			/			

Name: _____

Month: _____

Year: _____

Weight: _____

😊 😊 😊

This Month's Goals...

_____

_____

_____

Are You Drinking Enough Water?

Challenge yourself! Mark a raindrop each time you drink more water.

Great job

Keep going

You did good

Drink more next month.
Exercise and stretch daily.
Limit the suger you eat and drink.

MONTHLY PATIENT LOG SHEET

Day	✓	Pulse	Blood/Pressure	Temperature	Blood sugar 1	Blood sugar 2
1			/			
2			/			
3			/			
4			/			
5			/			
6			/			
7			/			
8			/			
9			/			
10			/			
11			/			
12			/			
13			/			
14			/			
15			/			
16			/			
17			/			
18			/			
19			/			
20			/			
21			/			
22			/			
23			/			
24			/			
25			/			
26			/			
27			/			
28			/			
29			/			
30			/			
31			/			

Diabetes and Polyneuropathy Awareness